Prickle I'm Sorry

written by
LISA WILKINSON
illustrated by
KATHI MCCORD

The Standard Publishing Company, Cincinnati, Ohio. A division of Standex International Corporation.
Text © 1999 by Lisa Wilkinson. Illustrations © 1999 by The Standard Publishing Company.
Cover design by Robert Glover.
Printed in the United States of America. All rights reserved.

06 05 04 03 02 01 00 99   5 4 3 2 1

Library of Congress Catalog Card Number 98-61300
ISBN 0-7847-0893-2
Scripture on page 24 quoted from the *International Children's Bible, New Century Version,*
© 1986, 1988 by Word Publishing, Dallas, Texas 75039. Used by permission.

STANDARD
PUBLISHING
Cincinnati, Ohio

Prickle, Cooper, Cotton, Sam, and Lulu
skated to the playground. They skated
to the big oak tree by the swings.
   Lulu bumped into Sam,
        who bumped into Cotton,
            who bumped into Cooper,
               who bumped into Prickle.

"Nobody likes Lulu. Pass it on," Prickle said to Cooper.
"Nobody likes Lulu. Pass it on," Cooper said to Cotton.
"Nobody likes Lulu. Pass it on," Cotton said to Sam.
"Nobody likes Lulu. Pass it on," Sam said to Lulu.
"Nobody likes me?" Lulu asked. Lulu lowered her head
and slowly skated home.

Prickle, Cooper, Cotton, and Sam slid down the slide.
Sam slid into Cotton,
who slid into Cooper,
who slid into Prickle.
"Nobody likes Sam. Pass it on," Prickle said to Cooper.
"Nobody likes Sam. Pass it on," Cooper said to Cotton.
"Nobody likes Sam. Pass it on," Cotton said to Sam.
"Nobody likes me?" Sam asked. Sam kicked at a rock
and slowly walked home.

Prickle, Cooper, and Cotton played jacks on the sidewalk.
   Cotton bounced the ball,
       which bounced past Cooper,
          and bounced past Prickle,
             and bounced into the sewer drain.
"Nobody likes Cotton. Pass it on," Prickle said to Cooper.
"Nobody likes Cotton. Pass it on," Cooper said to Cotton.
"Nobody likes me?" Cotton asked. Cotton picked up
her skates and plodded home.

Prickle and Cooper shot baskets on the basketball court.
Cooper stepped on Prickle's foot.
"Nobody likes Cooper. Pass it on," Prickle said to Cooper.
"Nobody likes me?" Cooper asked.
    Cooper put on his skates,
        tucked his basketball under his arm,
            and slowly skated home.

Prickle looked around the playground.
She looked at the swings.
    She looked at the slide.
        She looked at the sidewalk.
            She looked at the basketball court.
Lulu was gone.
    Sam was gone.
        Cotton was gone.
            Cooper was gone.
                Prickle was all alone.

Prickle skated to
Cooper's house.
Cooper was sitting on
his front porch steps.

"I'm sorry, Cooper," said Prickle. "I do like you."
"I like you, too," said Cooper. "I'm sorry I stepped
on your foot."
Prickle smiled. Cooper smiled.

They skated to Cotton's house.
Cotton was on her tire swing.

"We're sorry, Cotton," said Prickle and
Cooper. "We do like you."
"I like you, too," said Cotton. "I'm sorry
I lost the ball."
    Prickle smiled.
        Cooper smiled.
            Cotton smiled.

They skated to Sam's house. Sam was in his yard,
digging a hole with a stick.
"We're sorry, Sam," said Prickle, Cooper, and Cotton.
"We do like you."

"I like you, too," said Sam. "I'm sorry I slid into you."
Prickle smiled.
Cooper smiled.
Cotton smiled.
Sam smiled.

They skated to Lulu's house. Lulu
looked down from her tree house.
"We're sorry, Lulu," said Prickle, Cooper,
Cotton, and Sam. "We do like you."
"I like you, too," said Lulu. "I'm sorry I
bumped into you."
　　Prickle smiled. Cooper smiled.
　　　Cotton smiled. Sam smiled.
　　　　Lulu smiled.

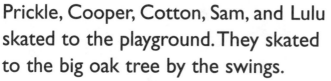

Prickle, Cooper, Cotton, Sam, and Lulu
skated to the playground. They skated
to the big oak tree by the swings.
Lulu tripped and fell into Sam,
who tripped and fell into Cotton,
who tripped and fell into Cooper,
who tripped and fell into Prickle,
who tripped and fell on the sidewalk.

"Nobody likes—" Prickle said.
Prickle looked at Cooper.
She looked at Cotton.
She looked at Sam.
She looked at Lulu.
Cooper, Cotton, Sam, and Lulu looked back at Prickle.
"Nobody likes," Prickle said again. "Nobody likes—"

"Nobody likes to fall down!"
Prickle and Cooper and Cotton and Sam and Lulu
laughed
and laughed
and laughed.

"Be kind and loving to each other. Forgive each other just as God forgave you in Christ."
—Ephesians 4:32